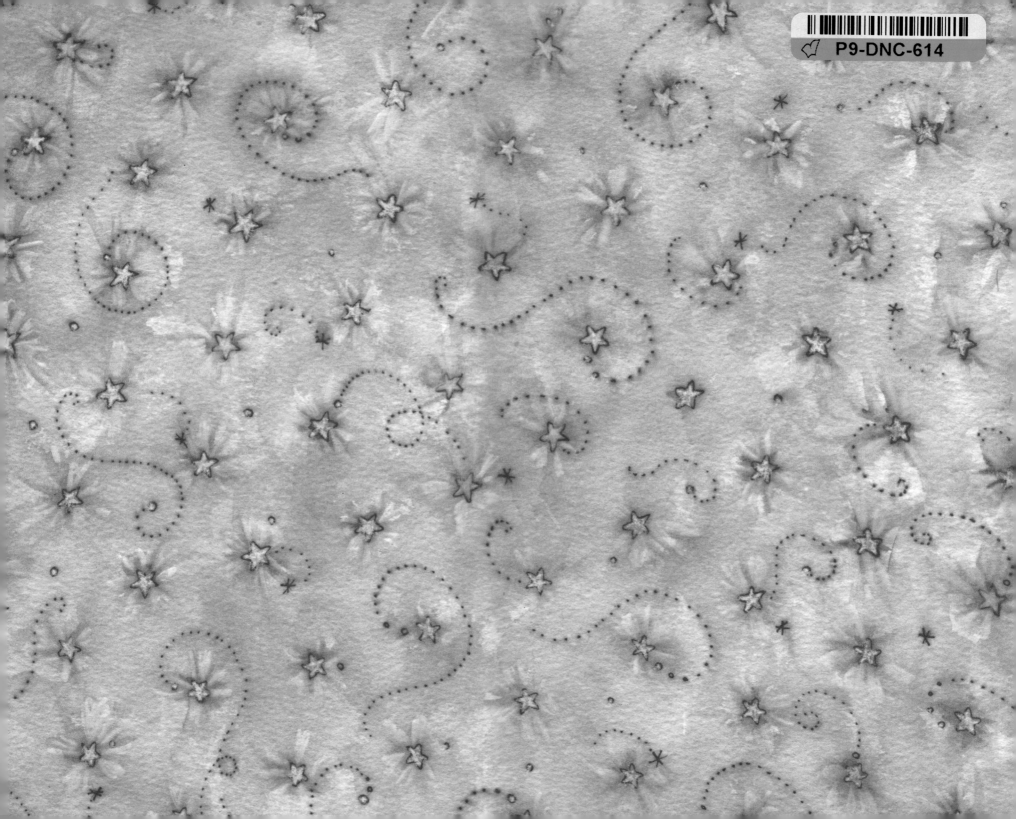

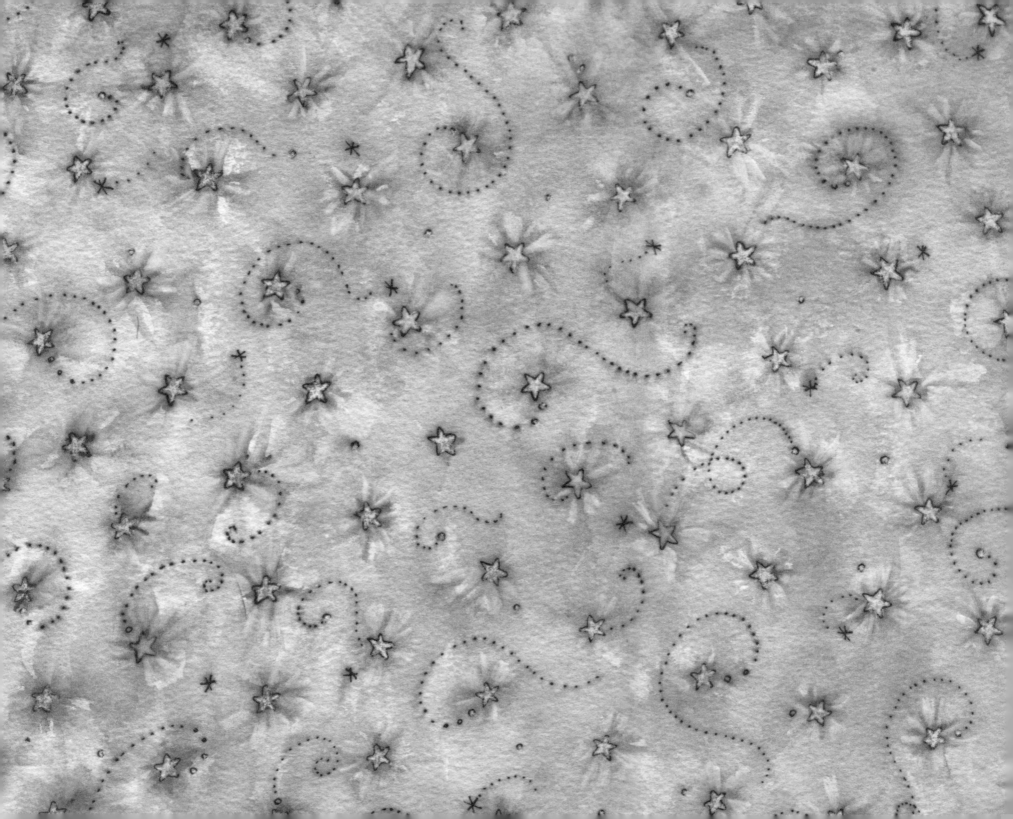

THE KNOT FAIRY

BY BOBBIE HINMAN

ILLUSTRATED BY KRISTI BRIDGEMAN

DESIGN AND LAYOUT BY JEFF URBANCIC

To Sydney ~
Always believe in fairies !
Bobbie Hinman
2009

Best Fairy Books

www.bestfairybooks.com

The Knot Fairy

Copyright © 2007 Bobbie Hinman
Illustrations by Kristi Bridgeman, 2007 © CARCC, 2007

Voices on CD: Narrator, Bobbie Hinman; Vocalist, Michele Block; Guitarist, Michael Block;
Children, Granddaughters - Lindsay, Emily, Kaitlyn, Jordan

Text design and layout: Jeff Urbancic
Audio engineer: William Whiteford

Library of Congress Control Number: 2006907531

Publisher's Cataloging-in-Publication
(Provided by Quality Books, Inc.)

Hinman, Bobbie.
   The knot fairy / by Bobbie Hinman ; illustrations by Kristi Bridgeman.
   p. cm. + 1 sound disc (digital ; 4 3/4 in.)
   Includes compact disc.
   Compact disc: Narrator, Bobbie Hinman ; vocalist, Michele Block;
guitar, Michael Block.
   SUMMARY: In this rhyming book, a playful little fairy, dressed in pajamas
 and fuzzy slippers, visits children while they sleep and delights in tangling their hair.
   Audience: Ages 3-7.
   ISBN-13: 978-0-9786791-0-1
   ISBN-10: 0-9786791-0-5

   1. Fairies--Juvenile fiction. 2. Hair--Juvenile
fiction. 3. Sleep--Juvenile fiction. [1. Fairies--
Fiction. 2. Hair--Fiction. 3. Sleep--Fiction.
4. Stories in rhyme.]   I. Bridgeman, Kristi, ill. II. Title.

PZ8.3.H5564Kno 2007   [E]
                  QBI06-600327

For information: www.bestfairybooks.com

This book is dedicated with love, to my precious grandchildren.
After all, they introduced me to the Knot Fairy.

And, to all children who wake up in the morning with knots in their hair.
You're not the only ones!

Do you believe in fairies who live in a magical space?

Lots of cute fairies with bright colored wings
may be hiding all over the place.

Shhhhhhhhhhhhhhhhhhhhhhhhh

hhhhhhhhhhhhhhhhhhhhhhhhhhhhhhhh . . .

Now, I don't know if this is true.
It was told to me and I'll tell it to you.

It's about a fairy with knots in her hair. She visits children everywhere.

How To
Tie Knots
In Hair

She carries a lantern and a little blue book.

She's in her pajamas. Come! Let's take a look…

When evening comes and you turn off the light...

it's time to climb into bed for the night.

Your teeth are sparkling. Your hair is brushed.

And all through the house is a quiet hushhhhhhhhhhhhhhhhh...

But while you're sleeping, here's a funny thing…

a tiny fairy with purple wings…

flies into your room and heads for your bed.

She flaps her wings and lands right on your head!

Now here's a secret that I will share...

she just likes to tangle your hair!

She ties little knots, one after another,

then flitters away to your sister or brother.

And when she's all through, as quiet as a mouse...

she flaps her wings and leaves your house.

She visits most all little boys and girls...

whether their hair is straight or full of curls.

So, if your hair goes this way and that...

and you're thinking of hiding it under a hat...

just look in the mirror and shout with glee,

"It looks like the Knot Fairy visited me!"

The Knot Fairy Song
(To the tune of Twinkle, Twinkle Little Star)

I see a light up in the sky.
Is that a fairy flying by?

With her lantern glowing bright,
I can see its shining light.

I see a light up in the sky.
Is that a fairy flying by?

I see a light up in the sky.
It WAS a fairy flying by.

Smiling, landing in my hair,
Knots and tangles everywhere.

I see a light up in the sky.
It WAS the Knot Fairy flying by!

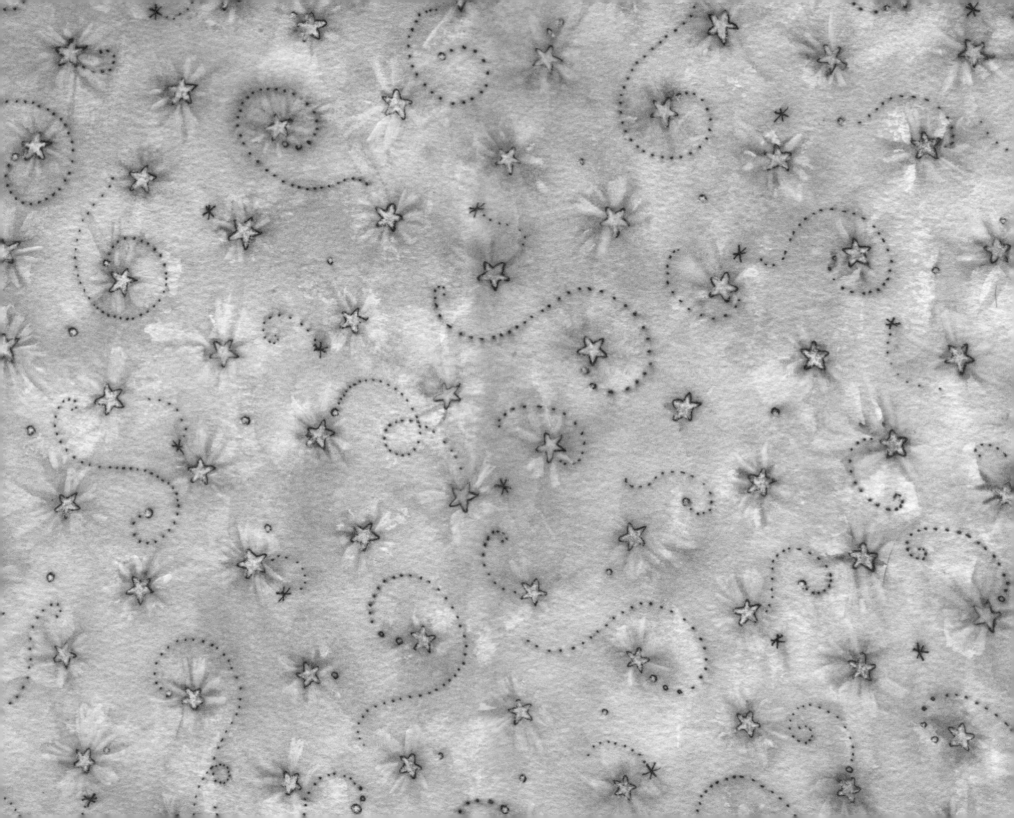

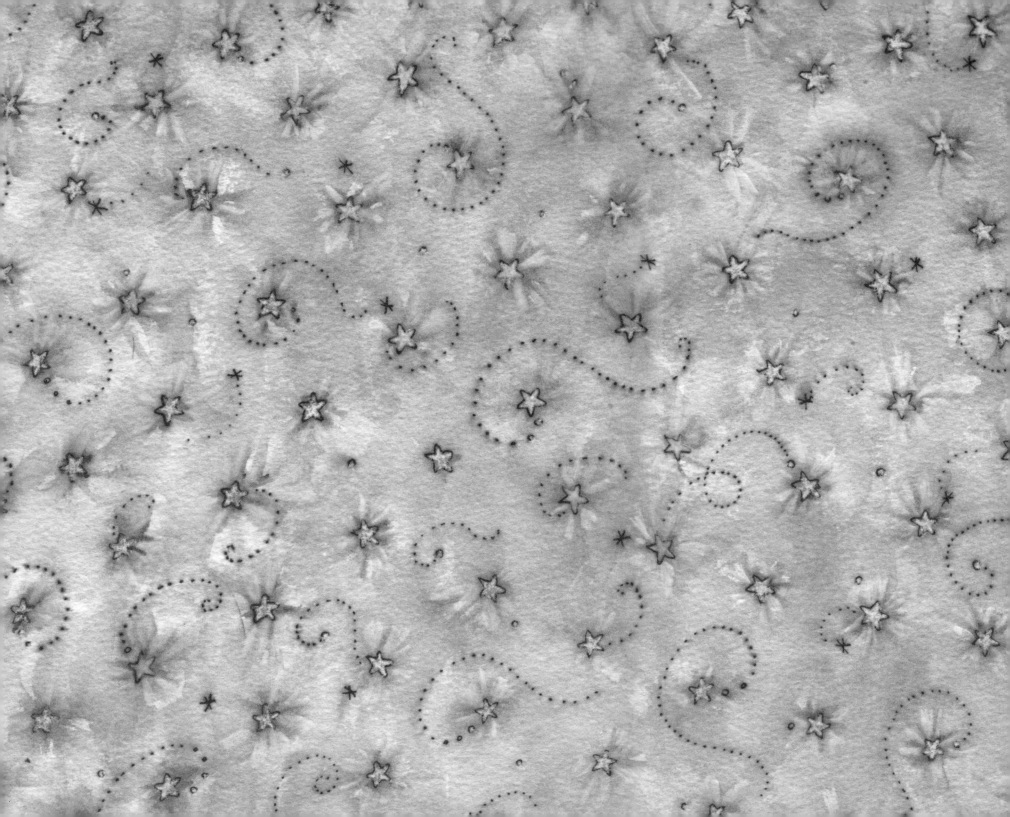